Perfectly
P⊛PPY

Poppy's New Puppy

story by Michele Jakubowski

pictures by Erica-Jane Waters

Curious
Fox

First published in the UK by Curious Fox,
an imprint of Capstone Global Library Limited,
7 Pilgrim Street, London, EC4V 6LB
Registered company number: 6695582

www.curious-fox.com

Illustrations by Erica-Jane Waters
All characters in this publication are fictitious and any resemblance to real persons,
living or dead, is purely coincidental.

ISBN 978 1 782 02198 8
19 18 17 16 15
10 9 8 7 6 5 4 3 2 1

A CIP catalogue for this book is available from the British Library.

Image credits: Shutterstock
Designer: Kristi Carlson

Printed in China by Nordica
0914/CA21401512

Table of Contents

Chapter 1

A Fluffy Puppy

"That's the one!" Poppy shouted. She was pointing at a fluffy, white puppy.

Poppy had wanted a puppy for a long time. She had asked her parents for one every day. On her birthday, they had finally said yes! Poppy was thrilled.

"Are you sure that's the one you want?" Poppy's mum asked.

Poppy put her face near the cage. The puppy licked her.

"Yes, I'm sure!" Poppy said.

Poppy's dad took the puppy
out of its cage. He placed it in
Poppy's arms. Poppy had never
been so happy!

"Now remember, Poppy,
puppies need a lot of attention,"
her dad said.

"I know," Poppy said. She
hugged the little ball of fur in her
arms. "We'll play together every
single day!"

"Do you have a name picked out?" Poppy's mum asked.

"Rosie," Poppy said. "Her name is Rosie."

Chapter 2

Rosie Rules

A few days later, Poppy and her best friend, Mille, were trying to watch their favourite TV programme. But Rosie was making that hard to do. She kept jumping and barking.

"Quiet, Rosie!" Poppy said.

Just then, Poppy's mum came

into the room.

"Rosie wants to play," she said.

"Puppies have a lot of energy. They

need a lot of activity. Why don't

you take her out into the garden?"

"Fine," Poppy said, but she wasn't happy about it.

She turned off the TV. She didn't like missing her favourite TV programme, but she had promised to take care of Rosie.

When they got outside, Poppy

and Millie sat on the ground.

Rosie danced around them.

"What do you play with her?"

Millie asked.

"I don't know," Poppy said.

"I've tried lots of games, but she

doesn't know how to play any

of them."

Poppy threw a ball into the yard. Rosie barked and chased after it. A short while later she came back to Poppy without the ball.

"See?" Poppy asked. "She never brings it back."

"I guess she has her own rules," Millie said.

"She has Rosie rules," Poppy said, laughing.

Millie thought for a moment. "Maybe she doesn't know that you want her to bring it back."

"You're right!" Poppy jumped

to her feet. "We need to teach her!"

Chapter 3

Good Girl

"You throw the ball, and I'll

go get it," Poppy said to Millie.

"Okay," Millie said. She threw

the ball far into the garden.

"Let's go, Rosie!" Poppy

shouted. She ran after the ball.

Rosie ran beside her.

When they got to the ball,

Poppy said, "Pick it up, Rosie!"

Rosie looked up at Poppy

and barked. She did not pick up

the ball.

"Like this," Poppy said. She picked up the ball. Rosie jumped up to get it from Poppy.

"Yes! Now you're getting it," Poppy said.

She let Rosie put the ball in
her mouth. She tried to get it
back, but Rosie held on tight.

"Rosie, drop the ball," Poppy
said. To her surprise, Rosie
dropped the ball.

"She's getting it!" Millie said.

"Good girl, Rosie," Poppy said.

"Let's try throwing it again,"

Millie said. "This time I'll chase

after it with Rosie."

Poppy, Millie and Rosie ran
around the garden chasing the
ball. They had so much fun!

"How about a snack break?"

Poppy's mum called.

Poppy and Millie sat at the

kitchen table munching on apples.

"Good news! I think Rosie finally knows how to play fetch," Poppy told her mum.

"It must be a lot of hard work learning a new game," Poppy's mum said.

Poppy and Millie looked under the table. Rosie was curled up on the floor sound asleep.

"It sure is!" they laughed.

Poppy's Diary

Dear Diary,

Today I had so much fun playing with Rosie. Millie and I taught her how to play fetch.

I've promised to play with her every day and help take care of her. I'm also going to try hard to be patient with her if she takes a while to learn something.

Next I'm going to teach her to roll over!

Poppy

Game Time!

I played fetch with Rosie, but there are lots of different games to play with a dog. If you don't have a dog, play these games with a friend. Be sure to reward your dog when he/she does something the right way. If you want, you can reward your friend, too!

Blanket hurdles

Make an obstacle course by using blankets or towels. Just roll up your blankets or towels and show your dog how to jump over them. If you are playing with a friend, you can time each other.

Simon says

If your dog knows the basic commands of sit, stay, down, roll over and shake, this game is for you! Test your dog's listening skills by calling out the commands. If you are playing with a friend, be sure to actually say "Simon says," which you won't say when playing with your pup.

Grab your dog's favourite ball and a laundry basket. Show your dog how to drop the ball into the basket when you say "drop." It might take a few tries, but your dog will soon understand how to make a basket. If you are playing with a friend, see who can make the most shots. Make it fun by doing silly tricks like turning in circles before you throw or throwing with your eyes closed.

Perfectly POPPY

The Big Bike £3.99
9781782022008

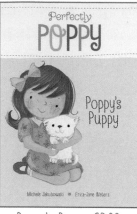

Poppy's Puppy £3.99
9781782021988

Football Star £3.99
9781782021995

Outside Surprise £3.99
9781782022015

Read all of Poppy's adventures!
Available from all good booksellers.